MW01178825

CONQUERING BULIMIA

CONQUERING EATING DISORDERS™

CONQUERING BULIMIA

URSULA DREW AND STEPHANIE WATSON

ROSEN
PUBLISHING®

New York

Published in 2016 by The Rosen Publishing Group, Inc.
29 East 21st Street, New York, NY 10010

First Edition

Library of Congress Cataloging-in-Publication Data

Drew, Ursula.
 Conquering bulimia / Ursula Drew and Stephanie Watson. – First edition.
     pages cm. – (Conquering eating disorders)
 Audience: Grades 7-12.
 Includes bibliographical references and index.
 ISBN 978-1-4994-6201-2 (library bound)
 1. Bulimia–Juvenile literature. 2. Eating disorders–Juvenile literature. I.
 Watson, Stephanie, 1969- II. Title.
 RC552.B84D74 2016
 616.85'263–dc23

                           2015013272

For many of the images in this book, the people photographed are models. The depictions do not imply actual situations or events.

Manufactured in the United States of America

CONTENTS

What Is an Eating Disorder?

CHAPTER ONE

An eating disorder is marked by an unhealthy relationship with food. This might mean that a person diets or exercises excessively, as someone with the eating disorder anorexia nervosa might do. It may mean patterns of extreme eating (also called bingeing) followed by compensating for overeating such as purging, as some people who have bulimia nervosa may do. It may simply be periods of overeating, which plagues people who have binge eating disorder.

Eating disorders are more than just problems with food. Having negative feelings about food can seriously affect not only how you eat but also how you interact with your friends, family, and everyone else around you. Your unhealthy relationship with food can harm both your body and your emotions.

In this resource, we will be focused on the disorder bulimia nervosa. The word *bulimia* comes from the Greek words *buos* ("ox") and *limos* ("hunger"), which together mean "hunger of an ox." People who have bulimia eat a lot of food at once (called bingeing) and then try to get rid of that food (called purging) so that they don't gain weight.

Eating disorders are more common than you might think. According to the National Eating Disorders Association, about five to ten million girls and women, and one million boys in the United States are battling eating disorders such as anorexia

Eating disorders like bulimia nervosa often manifest in secret.

nervosa and bulimia nervosa. And up to 15 percent of young women have unhealthy attitudes about food, reported www.girlpower.gov, a website sponsored by the U.S. Department of Health and Human Services. Although eating disorders are far more likely to affect young girls and women, about 5 to 15 percent of people with an eating disorder are male, according to the National Association of Anorexia Nervosa and Associated Disorders (ANAD).

The reasons why a person develops an eating disorder are complex. They involve eating habits, attitudes about weight and food, attitudes about body shape, and psychological factors, especially the need for control.

What Is Bulimia?

Although it was first diagnosed in the 1950s and was probably around even before then, bulimia nervosa wasn't really understood until the 1980s. Since then, we have learned of famous people who suffered from it, including Russell Brand, a UK stand-up comedian, television host, and actor, who started binge eating at age eleven, and American actress Lindsay Lohan. Both are also noted for having substance abuse problems, which often go hand in hand with eating disorders.

Today, bulimia is a major social concern. It can have devastating affects on the mind and body. Many eating disorder experts believe that images in the media put a lot of pressure on young men and women to reach an "ideal" body shape—one that is impossible for most people to achieve. Now parents, doctors, and school counselors are learning about the early warning signs of bulimia and other eating disorders in young people. Researchers are working to help people recover, but they also understand that more needs to be done to help prevent these harmful disorders in the first place.

Two Types of Bulimia

Bulimia nervosa is a type of eating disorder in which a person binges and purges. Bingeing means eating a large amount of food in a short period of time. Purging means getting rid of all the food by self-induced vomiting; abuse of laxatives, diet pills, and/or diuretics; excessive exercise; or fasting. Bingeing can mean eating a lot of calories—as many as 5,000 or more at a time. People with bulimia can binge once in a while, or twenty times each day or more. Then they will purge to rid their bodies of the extra calories. They may purge even after eating small amounts of food.

Purging can mean induced vomiting or abusing laxatives or diuretics to get rid of food.

The two types of bulimia are called purging and non-purging. People with the purging type get rid of food in different ways. Some people purge by self-inducing vomiting. Others use drugs, such as diuretics (pills that increase urination), diet pills, laxatives (usually mild drugs that induce bowel movements), or enemas (liquids injected into the anus for cleansing the bowels) to clear the digestive tract. Both bingeing and purging can be experienced as intense, overwhelming urges that become uncontrollable. People with the non-purging type of bulimia exercise compulsively to get rid of the extra food they've eaten or rely on fasting.

Who Suffers from Bulimia?

It is difficult to say exactly how many people suffer from bulimia because doctors are not required to report it to health agencies. In addition, many who suffer from bulimia do not seek help. ANAD reports that 47 percent of girls in fifth to twelfth grade want to lose weight because of the pictures they see in magazines, 42 percent of first to third grade girls report wanting to be thinner, and 81 percent of ten year olds fear becoming fat. Boys who are involved in activities that have them gain and lose weight quickly, such as wrestling and gymnastics, are most at risk. While most people who suffer from bulimia are in their late teens and early twenties, the disorder is affecting people at younger ages than ever before. Therapists also report an increase in the numbers of middle-aged women with the disease.

What Are the Symptoms?

It can be difficult to tell if a person has an eating disorder. Bulimia is especially tough to diagnose because the problem is often hidden.

Magazines targeted to women often present an unattainable image of beauty that makes readers feel badly about they way they look and contributes to eating disorders.

Many people struggle with their relationship to food. We are taught from an early age to feel anxious and guilty around food, when we are told to finish what's on our plate, or to worry about our weight and fear fat. People who are in the early stages of bulimia (or another eating disorder) may be overly concerned with their weight, but that isn't out of the ordinary in our culture.

People with bulimia are also not always really skinny. They can be of normal weight or even overweight.

Warning Signs

Even though people with bulimia may not look different from anyone else, there are warning signs of the condition. A person with the disorder may use extreme methods to lose weight and may act different from how he or she used to act. It's important to recognize these warning signs so that you can help yourself or help someone else who is struggling with bulimia. An eating disorder left untreated can be life threatening. People with bulimia may do one or more of these things:

- Believe that they would be happier and more successful if they were thinner
- Have severe mood swings
- Overeat in response to stress or other uncomfortable feelings
- Alternate between strict dieting and overeating
- Go to the bathroom a lot to throw up after eating
- Exercise all the time
- Buy or steal large amounts of food
- Buy certain products, such as laxatives or syrup of ipecac (used to induce vomiting)
- Have cuts or marks on their knuckles and fingertips from using their fingers to induce vomiting
- Show other types of impulsive behavior, such as abusing drugs, going on shopping sprees, and/or shoplifting

Bulimia and Anorexia

Although they are different disorders, anorexia and bulimia share many of the same symptoms. This is the reason why "nervosa" is part of both terms. In fact, about 50 percent of people who have bulimia had anorexia first. In both cases, the person is preoccupied with dieting, food, weight, and body size. But there are also a few differences. People with anorexia refuse to eat. They also deny that there is a problem to themselves and to others. People with bulimia usually eat but then purge. They are aware that there is a problem, even though they may try to keep it a secret from others. People with anorexia are 15 percent below the recommended weight for their size. Those with bulimia are usually of average weight, though they may weigh 10 or 15 pounds (4.5 or 6.8 kilograms) above or below the average.

The Emotional Side of Bulimia

When people purge, they are not just getting rid of food. They are also trying to get rid of unwanted feelings, like anxiety, anger, guilt, panic, and stress. And it doesn't take very long for the bingeing and purging habit to become an addictive pattern.

Although scientists are still researching this idea, some believe purging may affect chemicals in the brain, causing a person to feel satisfied after an episode. Comedian Russell Brand mentioned that he felt "euphoric" after purging. A person with bulimia repeats the cycle to feel the same rush after purging. They believe that purging is the only way to get those feelings again. Bulimia turns the act of eating into a self-destructive behavior. Eating stops being a pleasurable experience. Food is instead used to deal with uncomfortable feelings like fear, anger, and guilt. People with bulimia are unable to stop the secret cycle of bingeing and purging because they rely upon this ritual to handle their feelings. Soon it has taken over their lives. No matter how thin they are, people with bulimia always fear that they will get fat. They feel that being thin means being happy.

People with bulimia often have a distorted view of themselves and see their bodies as being much larger than they actually are.

People with bulimia are unable to deal with uncomfortable feelings. They see their bodies as being much larger than they really are. As a result, they refuse to eat in a healthy way and use dangerous methods to lose weight.

Who Is at Risk?

While the majority of bulimia sufferers are women between the ages of twelve and twenty-five, usually from upper middle-class families, this is an eating disorder that can affect anyone. Western society puts a lot of pressure on young people to look thin because of the media stereotypes of beauty. Both men and women of any age and every economic group can be affected by these images and, coupled with other factors, can develop an eating disorder like bulimia. Popularity, wealth, race, or IQ have no bearing on who may develop an eating disorder. The main factor is how people feel about themselves and what they look like. Remember that people who suffer with bulimia nervosa may appear to have an average weight or may even be overweight. Unlike anorexia, where the person can become extremely thin, people suffering from bulimia can easily hide among a crowd. People who have drug or alcohol problems may be at higher risk than others, as well as people who connect weight with performance, such as dancers or athletes. Because many people think of this as a "female problem," some young men may be too embarrassed to tell anyone about it and get the help they need. However, more and more men of all ages are being affected by this disorder.

MYTHS and *FACTS*

MYTH Only young, upper-class white females become bulimic.

 Bulimia affects people from all walks of life, of all races and genders.

MYTH Purging will help me to stay thin.

 Many people with bulimia are at or over what is considered "normal" weight.

MYTH Bulimia is harmless.

 People who binge and purge create stresses on their body that make it difficult for them to recover from other illnesses. In addition, the nutrients lost during purging can also cause low potassium or an electrolyte imbalance, which can cause the heart to stop beating. The death rate for people with eating disorders is about 20 percent.

MYTH Bulimia runs in the family.

 There is some indication that a person's biology can make them predisposed to bulimia. And some people may be also predisposed to having this disorder because others in their family have it, and in turn, they create a culture of body criticism that can lead to this disorder. However, life changes and stressful events can also be a main factor in whether a person develops bulimia.

MYTH If you have bulimia, you can't recover from it.

 With treatment, most people can recover from bulimia. The sooner you get help, the better your chances of recovery. Some people who have undergone treatment for bulimia have been able to recover fully.

CHAPTER TWO

The Effects of Bulimia

Bulimia can have devastating effects on your body and mind. This disorder can adversely affect everything from your hormones, your blood, and organs like your heart and kidneys to damaging your skin.

Physical Effects of Bulimia

Bulimia can damage almost every organ in the body. People with bulimia may suffer from anemia, an irregular heartbeat, weakened muscles, low blood pressure, dehydration, low nutrient levels, and compromised organs such as the skin, heart, brain, and kidneys. It is important to note that the longer bulimia remains untreated, the worse the problems become.

Health Problems

About half of the women with bulimia have an irregular menstrual cycle (period) or stop having their period altogether, according to the American Academy of Family Physicians. Not getting a period is called amenorrhea. Studies have found that not menstruating can cause other problems as well. Women who don't get their periods lack enough estrogen, which helps maintain strong bones. A lack of estrogen can cause osteoporosis, a disease that weakens the

How bulimia affects your body

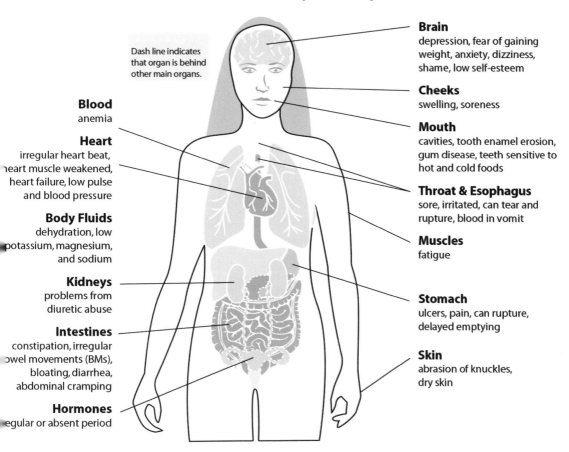

Dash line indicates that organ is behind other main organs.

Brain
depression, fear of gaining weight, anxiety, dizziness, shame, low self-esteem

Cheeks
swelling, soreness

Mouth
cavities, tooth enamel erosion, gum disease, teeth sensitive to hot and cold foods

Throat & Esophagus
sore, irritated, can tear and rupture, blood in vomit

Muscles
fatigue

Stomach
ulcers, pain, can rupture, delayed emptying

Skin
abrasion of knuckles, dry skin

Blood
anemia

Heart
irregular heart beat, heart muscle weakened, heart failure, low pulse and blood pressure

Body Fluids
dehydration, low potassium, magnesium, and sodium

Kidneys
problems from diuretic abuse

Intestines
constipation, irregular bowel movements (BMs), bloating, diarrhea, abdominal cramping

Hormones
irregular or absent period

This chart from *womenshealth.com* shows the many ways that bulimia negatively affects the body. Although the image is female, boys and men are also affected by bulimia.

bones. When the bones are weak, they break easily. Other health problems that can be caused by bulimia include:

- Irregular heartbeat
- Low blood pressure
- Dehydration
- Vitamin and mineral imbalances
- Irregular bowel movements
- Diarrhea
- Abdominal cramps
- Dizziness
- Swelling of the cheeks
- Gum disease
- Cavities (erosion of tooth enamel)
- Sore throat and esophagus due to stomach acid
- Cuts on knuckles (from biting the skin with the teeth during induced vomiting)

Athletes and Bulimia

For some female athletes, bulimia can cause a condition that doctors call the female athlete triad. The word *triad* refers to the three health problems that occur together in many female athletes: disordered eating, loss of menstrual periods, and loss of bone mass. Any one of these conditions can signal that the body's essential nutrients and tissues are being raided, usually by a combination of starvation and over-exercising.

When all three conditions appear at the same time, it is a health emergency. Experts aren't sure exactly how many women have the female athlete triad. But a British study found that as many as 15 to 60 percent of female athletes in sports such as gymnastics, long-distance running, and figure skating have disordered eating, and as many as 50 percent of these women over-exercise.

Losing Vitamins and Minerals

When you vomit after eating, you lose the vitamins, minerals, and other nutrients that would normally be absorbed into your body. Not eating normally can throw your body into emergency mode. After a few days, you will start using up your fat deposits and then

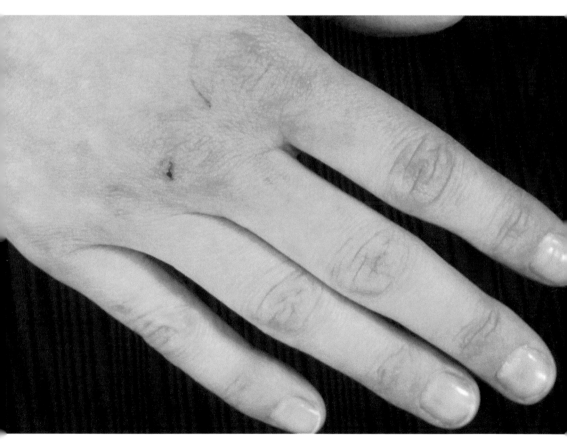

Cuts on a person's knuckles may indicate a problem with the purging type of bulimia. However, this is coupled with several other signs that indicate an eating disorder.

muscle. To keep going, your body will rob nutrients from organs such as the liver and heart. You also lose water when you vomit, which can lead to dehydration.

Dehydration from purging causes dry skin, brittle nails and hair, and hair loss. A lack of vitamins and minerals such as iron, phosphorous, and potassium in the body can put a person at risk for malnutrition even if that person is not too thin and eats regular meals at other times. Not having enough of these vitamins and minerals can make a person feel tired. It can also cause skin problems, weak eyesight, and damage to the heart, kidneys, and bones.

The most serious side effect of bulimia is an electrolyte imbalance. Repeated purging causes a depletion of the electrolytes potassium, chlorine, and sodium. These are electrically charged ions necessary for all of the body's major systems to function. An electrolyte imbalance can cause kidney problems, muscle spasms, heart irregularities, and even death.

Stomach and Organ Trouble

Vomiting is a violent reflex that batters the esophagus and stomach lining. The damage is invisible, but it is so serious that it can become painful to swallow anything, even water.

Over time, it gets hard to keep any food down. The body will purge as an automatic reflex after eating. In severe cases, the lining of the esophagus will wear away. A hole in the esophagus can cause sudden death. All of this stomach damage from purging can cause pain, cramps, and indigestion. Using laxatives can also cause painful spasms in the intestines, and using them too often can actually make a person constipated to the point that they depend on laxatives to have normal bowel movements.

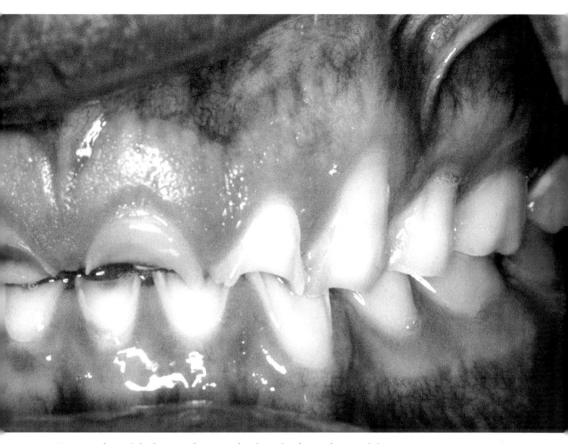

Stomach acids brought up during induced vomiting can wear down the teeth. It makes a person more susceptible to tooth decay and other oral diseases.

What Bulimia Looks Like on the Outside

Not only does bulimia cause problems inside the body, it also leaves more obvious symptoms on the outside. The pressure of repeated vomiting can cause blood vessels in the face (especially in and around the eyes), legs, and arms to break, leaving little red lines in the skin. Purging can also cause puffiness and swelling in the hands, feet, or face. And purging can cause the salivary glands in the face to enlarge, making the cheeks look swollen. Vomiting over and over brings stomach acids up into the mouth. These acids are strong enough to break down foods. They are also strong enough to wear away tooth enamel and the softer tissues of the mouth. They can leave holes or raggedy edges in the teeth and can make the gums swollen and tender. People who vomit a lot are likely to develop tooth decay and gum disease, and could lose many teeth.

Using laxatives can cause repeated diarrhea. This can lead to a condition called rectal prolapse, in which part of your colon comes out through your rectum. It may need to be fixed surgically.

Mental and Emotional Effects

When all of your time and energy is focused on weight and what you are or aren't eating, it can take a big emotional toll on your life. It can affect your relationships with your family and friends, and make you miss out on the things you once loved to do.

Emotional Pain

People suffering from bulimia often feel guilty and ashamed. Bingeing and purging can cause intense and overwhelming feelings of anxiety and tension. There is also fear when people realize they are hurting their bodies. Most frightening of all is the belief that there is no way to make it all stop.

Bulimia can have a big effect on personality. Many people who have bulimia have mood swings. They may be happy and upbeat when they feel in control, then hopeless and depressed when they feel like they've eaten too much or lost control. The depression that often comes with bulimia can drain them of their energy and make them stay home alone rather than going out with friends.

Some people spend a lot of time focused on what they are putting into their bodies. This can be a good thing if they are thinking about nutrition, but bulimics often think only of calories.

Compulsive Behaviors

Some people who have eating disorders also have compulsive behaviors that affect their eating. These are also called rituals. Rituals can take many forms, but they are always habitual with each meal. Some rituals include cutting food into tiny morsels or moving food around the plate without actually eating any of it. Another ritual might be to binge eat and then purge or to go to the bathroom immediately after a meal. Hiding food and over-exercising are also considered rituals if they are habitual. People with bulimia become very protective of their rituals. These behaviors give them a sense of control. However, they are really not in control of what and how they eat. People with bulimia have a distorted self-image because they often have little contact with other people. They may also be very depressed about what they are doing to themselves. These feelings can be devastating. In the worst cases, a person may consider suicide as the only way out. That's why it's so important that a person with bulimia talks to someone that he or she trusts so that the person can get immediate help.

How and Why Does a Person Develop Bulimia?

CHAPTER THREE

There is no one cause for an eating disorder like bulimia. Factors range from a person's biology, to their home environment, depression, substance abuse, and negative self-image. Sudden

The number of boys and men affected by bulimia is on the rise, in some part, as a result of growing muscularity in action figures.

and drastic life changes can also trigger an eating disorder like bulimia. The source can be a combination of factors, making finding a reason even more complicated. This does not mean that everyone who overeats at some point or another, feels overwhelmed, or has a big life change will develop this disorder. We all have trying times, and even occasional overeating is normal. The difference is that someone with bulimia will do it on a regular basis and cannot control the urge to binge. The person who is experiencing it usually does not consciously decide to develop an eating disorder. It's an unconscious process.

An eating disorder is actually an expression of other problems in a person's life. It may be a way for people to feel some sense of control. It may be a way for them to feel a sense of identity, independence, or even security. It may be a way for them to compulsively repeat abusive situations, that is, to take in painful amounts of food while being able to then say "no" and to purge.

Other Triggers

Bulimia, as well as other eating disorders, tends to be triggered by family and relationship problems. It can start as a result of a comment about your weight from a parent or a friend, or if you're an athlete, the comment may come from a coach. Bulimia can also be a symptom of a larger problem, such as depression, low self-esteem, sexual abuse, or family dysfunction. Bulimia usually develops during big life changes such as a divorce, moving to another town, changing schools, or going off to college. It could also be a trauma, such as rape or sexual assault. Dramatic experiences that happen during the teen years, when young people are already experiencing major changes in their bodies, could trigger an eating disorder.

Images in the Media

One of the main issues that eating disorder experts agree on is the negative influence magazines, advertising, and television have on body image. Constantly seeing images of perfect models—which are often doctored in magazines and even on television—can have harmful effects on a person's self-esteem. The problem is that movies, television, and all forms of advertising make people feel that there is an ideal way their bodies should look. Everywhere you look, from billboards to TV ads, there is pressure to diet and be thin. Americans spend billions of dollars each year on dieting, from weight-loss centers to diet pills and diet books. Advertisers constantly try to convince us, with ads for everything from diet sodas to bathing suits, that if you eat, you'll get fat. And for many people, there is nothing worse than being fat.

One survey by the National Eating Disorders Association (NEDA) reported that young girls are more afraid of becoming fat than they are of cancer, nuclear war, or losing their parents. The media sends strong messages to young women that they are fat no matter what size they happen to be. As a result, many women and girls, and an increasing number of boys and men, have a distorted body image. They think they need to lose weight, when in fact, they are very healthy at their current body size.

There has been a lot of backlash recently about the negative image the media sends to women, and some are taking notice. In 2006, Spain banned models that were too skinny from the fashion catwalks. That was followed up by a law against models with a low body mass index (BMI) in 2013, with both Italy and Israel also signing laws to that effect. In 2015, France, the capital of the fashion industry, is also set to enforce regular weight checks for models. This comes after the 2007 death of French fashion model Isabelle Caro, who suffered from anorexia nervosa.

Some studies have shown that a healthy body image can be promoted by viewing images of all different kinds of body types.

Family Matters

Research has shown that young children will eat only when they're hungry. They naturally control how much they eat. But parents soon interfere with their children's eating patterns.

When this happens, children learn to eat for reasons other than hunger. Parental influence makes food take on a different meaning. For example, you learn at a young age what is okay to eat after school or what is not allowed before dinner. You may be told that candy and other sweets are "bad" for you but you are given them as rewards for "good" behavior.

Parents influence their children's eating in other ways. Sometimes, parents who are concerned about their own weight cause their children to worry about their weight, too. Or, a mother may keep telling her daughter that she has to be thinner to look good. One study found that 40 percent of nine- to ten-year-old girls lose weight when their mothers ask them to do so. A 2013 study in the *Journal of American Medicine* found that "mothers and fathers who engaged in weight-related conversations had adolescents who were more likely to diet, use unhealthy weight-control behaviors, and engage in binge-eating." The conclusion of the study was that "parent conversations focused on weight/size are associated with increased risk for adolescent disordered eating behaviors, whereas conversations focused on healthful eating are protective against disordered eating behaviors."

Bulimia may also run in families. A March 2006 study of 31,000 twins in Sweden revealed that there is a genetic component to an eating disorder like anorexia disorder. The study did not prove that binge eating is a result of genes, but it did prove that binge eating does tend to happen in family groups. The study concluded that "eating disorders are familial disorders."

Drugs and Alcohol

Research shows that people with eating disorders are more likely to have parents who abuse alcohol or drugs. In a home in which a parent is an alcoholic or drug abuser, children live in an almost constant state of disorder. They may never know from one minute to the next how their parent will act. They may be afraid to have friends visit. They may spend lots of time alone taking care of themselves. An eating disorder may be a cry for help in this lonely

Family trauma such as drug and alcohol abuse can contribute to eating disorders in children.

situation. Or, it may be a way for them to take control of some part of their life—over what they eat, how much they eat, and even how they rid their body of food.

Physical and Sexual Abuse

Childhood sexual and physical abuse have also been linked to eating disorders. In a 2008 study, 12.1 percent of women with bulimia reported an incident of sexual abuse before the age of sixteen. Slightly over 8 percent of women with bulimia reported two or more such incidents. The abusers might have been a parent, a friend, a relative, or another trusted adult. The betrayal and pain that comes from being abused can lead to severe emotional problems. The eating disorder can be a way to bury those painful feelings and ease the emotional pain. People who are sexually abused grow up with little or no sense of control over their own bodies. Bulimia is an attempt to regain control. Bulimia in the case of abuse may also be a way for people to punish themselves because they feel they don't deserve to be happy. When people don't feel worthy enough to express what they want, they can start bingeing and purging behaviors. Bingeing is a way to express their desires, and purging is like punishing themselves for trying to fulfill those desires.

Self-Destructive Behavior

How you feel about yourself and your body can affect your eating habits. People who have bulimia may have certain personality traits that lead to destructive eating behaviors.

One trait is perfectionism: wanting to do everything just right and being very hard on yourself if you make a mistake. Another trait is self-loathing: you see a fat, ugly person every time you look in the mirror, even if everyone else sees you as thin and pretty. Many people with bulimia are also depressed. They feel sad a lot, and they withdraw from family and friends.

Dieting

What happens when people feel that they're not good enough because they're not thin enough? They usually think a diet is the answer to all their problems. But diets are dangerous because they set up an unhealthy relationship with food. In fact, while not all diets lead to eating disorders, adolescents who are serious dieters are

Excessive dieting or using medication to help purge your system can be very dangerous to the body.

eighteen times more likely to develop an eating disorder than those who don't diet, according to the National Association of Anorexia Nervosa and Associated Disorders.

Diets are not always healthy. When people restrict their food intake, they are depriving themselves. This can cause them to become obsessed with everything they feel they are missing. It is natural for the body to rebel against a diet. When your body is deprived of food, it reacts as if it were being attacked. Your metabolism slows down, and your body burns fewer calories. This is because your body is trying to hold on to the little food it's getting. The body reacts to dieting by storing fat more efficiently to survive. When people with bulimia break their diets, they often binge. Breaking a diet can cause feelings of guilt. The only way to relieve that guilt is to purge.

Mental Health

Some eating disorders may begin with a small goal to lose weight and to eat better. But in some cases, those plans go very wrong, resulting in disorders such as bulimia. There is a link between people who have eating disorders and those who also have a history of depression. For example, according to the National Institute of Diabetes and Digestive and Kidney Diseases, as many as half of patients with binge eating disorder also have a history of depression. Depression can lead to feelings of hopelessness, which can lead to suicide. People with anorexia are 50 times more likely to die from suicide than a person in the general population.

A person with an eating disorder can become depressed, or a person who is depressed can develop an eating disorder. Life events can trigger depression, which can then lead to eating disorders, but malnutrition as a result of an eating disorder can also cause physiological changes that affect mood and lead to depression. Regardless of which triggers the eating disorder or the depression, the result is a vicious cycle that becomes more difficult to get out of once it begins. To determine whether depression is a part of an eating disorder, a doctor might ask you if you have feelings of sadness or unhappiness, if you have lost interest in things you used to enjoy, if you feel cranky or get angry easily, if you have trouble sleeping, or if you have lost your appetite. If you feel that you have depression along with, or as a result of, bulimia, talk to a doctor who can help you get the help you need.

Ending the Cycle of Bulimia

It may be difficult to deal with bulimia because of mixed messages in the media and from family, friends, or coaches. Some people with bulimia become caught in a cycle of behavior that makes it difficult to identify the signs of problems or, even when the signs are clear, make it hard to know what to do or whom to ask for help. Recovering from an eating disorder may not be easy, but it is possible with the right help. People dealing with bulimia need to find the right people to talk to so that they can learn to deal with issues, whether societal or personal, in a healthier way. The earlier you get help, the easier it will be to recover, but it is never too late to end the cycle.

Seek Professional Help

The most important thing to know about eating disorders is that you are not alone. Many people have suffered with this disorder, and there are many resources that can help you to get back to a healthier lifestyle. If you think you may suffer from bulimia or any eating disorder, it's extremely important to get professional help. Consider speaking with someone you trust, such as a parent, friend, or counselor. You can also contact one of the eating disorder organizations already mentioned in this resource or in the resources at the end for more information and help. Treating bulimia can be a long and complicated process. Some people who formerly suffered from bulimia

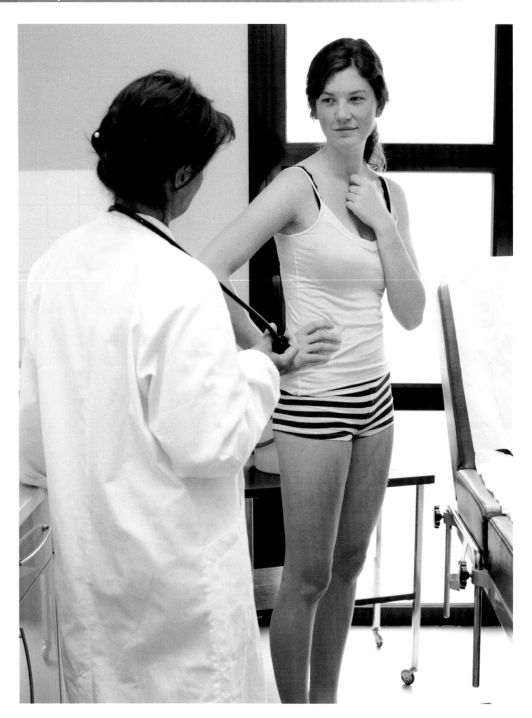

Once you recognize that you may have an eating disorder, it is important to seek medical help so that you can get better.

have said that recovering from bulimia was the toughest job they've ever had. It may take as long as six months to two years in treatment before a person can stop the binge-purge cycle. There is no specific time frame for recovery. It varies from person to person. However, the longer someone has had bulimia, the harder it is to break the habits. Once you recognize the problem, seek out help as soon as possible.

There are no laboratory tests specifically designed to detect bulimia, but a doctor may run tests to see what effects the eating disorder has had on the body. Blood tests can be done to check for potassium deficiency and other electrolyte imbalances. The doctor may also take a chest radiograph to look for signs that the esophagus has ruptured, an electrocardiogram to check how well the heart is working, and a thyroid test to make sure the thyroid gland is functioning properly.

Physical Health

There is no single way to recover from bulimia, and there are no miracle cures. You may have to try a few different types of treatment before one works for you. Although some people recover without therapy, most need some type of help. The first part of treatment for bulimia is to get your body healthy again. If the situation is a medical emergency, you may have to go to the hospital. This will happen if you are bingeing and purging several times every day, are dehydrated or have an electrolyte imbalance, or feel suicidal. You may be given fluids and nutrients through a vein in your arm until you are strong enough to eat on your own. Your doctor may give you an anti-nausea drug that will reduce your urge to vomit. You may also get an antacid to decrease stomach acids. And a nutritionist may work with you to get your eating back on a healthy track.

Getting Therapy

The first and most effective treatment for bulimia is behavioral therapy. Therapy can be done individually, with family, or in groups. A technique called cognitive-behavioral therapy is very effective for treating bulimia. This therapy helps people understand why they developed bulimia in the first place and teaches them how to change their thinking and behavior so that they can stop it from continuing. Because depression is common in people with bulimia, sometimes doctors prescribe drugs called antidepressants. These drugs help

Sometimes family therapy is necessary to help a person who is suffering from bulimia.

people deal with depression and other feelings bulimia can cause. Antidepressants should only be used by people who are of normal weight or who are overweight, though, because they can cause weight loss. The most common antidepressants are the selective serotonin reuptake inhibitors (SSRIs). These include Prozac, Zoloft, and Paxil. They work by affecting chemicals in the brain that are involved in mood.

Addressing Family Mental Health

The families of people with bulimia may need help healing, too. Family therapy can help improve relationships while the person with the eating disorder recovers. For families in which a problem such as abuse contributed to the eating disorder, treatment is even more important. Someone who is in recovery cannot get better if they continue to live with an abusive family. When a family problem, such as divorce or death, cannot be changed, the recovering person must learn new ways to cope.

Group Therapy

Talking to people who have had similar experiences can help you work through your feelings and come to terms with your disorder. This is called group therapy, or a support group. Group therapy can be a powerful process. Knowing you're not the only one with bulimia can help you feel less ashamed. It is also very comforting to be able to talk about your pain with people who will understand because they, too, have lived through it. Support groups are an important part of eating disorder treatment. There are many different types of support groups, and they are all very effective if the participants are willing to work hard to get well.

What to Do If a Loved One Has Bulimia

You may notice some of the warning signs of an eating disorder (binge eating, self-induced vomiting, perfectionist behavior) in a friend or relative. If you do, speak up. It may not be easy to do. It can feel as if you are betraying a loved one. But the person needs help. Set a time to talk and approach your friend or family member

If you notice the warning signs of an eating disorder in a friend or family member, talk to him or her. You may be able to steer the person toward the help he or she needs.

gently, tell him or her about your concerns, and listen sympatheti-cally. Try to understand that your friend may not admit she or he has a problem. If that happens, don't force your friend to get help. Give your friend support. Avoid placing blame or shaming the person, and don't oversimplify the problem by saying that they would be fine if they just stopped the behaviors you observed. Instead, ask questions and let them talk things through. Give the person a list of places to go for help or people to call, including the school guid-ance counselor. Even if your friend doesn't want help, he or she may keep the list and use it later. If your friend is not listening to you and you feel it is an emergency situation, confide in a trusted adult—a teacher, nurse, guidance counselor, friend, or family member. An emergency situation is if your friend is vomiting blood, has a very severe stomachache, vomits several times each day, or talks about suicide. Your friend may be angry, but you should react immediately because your friend's life is in danger.

How to Stay Healthy

Remember that bulimia is a chronic illness. Even with treatment, the condition can return. It is not easy to recover, but it is possible with help. If you are willing to help yourself, you'll have a better chance of recovering. Up to 20 percent of people who don't get treatment for eating disorders die, according to the National Association of Anorexia Nervosa and Associated Disorders (ANAD). With treat-ment, about 97 to 98 percent survive.

Recovering from Bulimia

ANAD has also indicated that about 60 percent of people with eat-ing disorders can recover if they get treatment. This is why receiving treatment is so important if you are suffering from bulimia. With treatment, you can learn how to eat well to keep your body at a healthy weight. You can get back into your regular routine with school, activities, and friends. Most of all, you can start to feel better about yourself.

Recovery Setbacks

Even with treatment, not everyone with bulimia will recover for good. Often people have many setbacks. As reported in 2006 by ANAD, just under half of the people with bulimia don't improve, or continue

It may be hard to choose between healthful eating and binge eating then purging. Therapy can help you make better decisions for a healthy body.

to have some problems throughout their lives. Some people recovering from bulimia will have to worry about relapse in the same way that a person with an addiction to alcohol must deal with relapse.

When people have a drug or alcohol addiction, the most important part of their treatment is to stop using those chemicals. They can avoid situations where they might be tempted to use them. But people with bulimia cannot stay away from food. They need to eat. A treatment program can help them learn to eat in a healthy way.

Relapse is a very real part of the recovery process. However, the chances for improvement are more positive than that for other eating disorders, such as anorexia.

CHAPTER FIVE

Prevention and Fighting Back

The first step in preventing or fighting an eating disorder is working to have a positive self-image. This may mean avoiding destructive media, such as television, web shows, magazines, and websites that promote an unhealthy or unattainable physical ideal. Knowing what are healthy portions of food and what kinds of foods are better for your body is also important in maintaining a healthy body and mind. You can find this information by talking to a parent, school counselor, or another person you trust. If you find that you are obsessing over food or your weight, then it may also be time to seek out someone to talk to about your concerns and why you have them before it becomes a bigger problem.

How to Prevent Bulimia

Harmful media messages that glorify being thin are hard to avoid, but remember that most magazines doctor photos so that people look different than they do in real life. Magazines regularly spend many hours working over photographs with a result that often bares little similarity to the original photograph.

With a little help from family, friends, doctors, and counselors, you can begin to love who you are right now, instead of who you wish you could be. There are many ways that you can fight back and help prevent eating disorders—both in yourself and in others.

Talk Through Your Emotions

If you are experiencing uncomfortable feelings or if something has changed in your life—your parents recently divorced, a family member is ill, or a good friend has moved away—don't hide your feelings. Find someone to talk to about what's on your mind. A school guidance counselor is a good place to start. Some towns have local hotlines for teens to call if they need someone to talk to. Some schools have peer support groups, so you can talk to your classmates about your concerns. Try to talk to your parents or anyone else you trust. Never keep your worries a secret.

Make Healthy Choices for Your Body

In addition to improving your mental outlook, you also need to take care of your body. It's not easy always to eat healthy foods. But making a real lifestyle change takes a bit of work. Fad diets, pills, and bingeing and purging offer quick fixes, but there are much healthier ways to lose weight and get in shape. The problem with fad diets and diet pills is they don't teach you to change your eating habits so that you eat right most of the time. If you eat a well-balanced diet that includes proteins, dairy, fruits, vegetables, and grains, your body will be healthy. And that's much more important than what the numbers say on your scale.

Remember your body shape and size is determined mostly by genetics. You have only so much control over what your body looks like. Look at yourself as an individual with very unique characteristics. Try not to compare yourself to an unrealistic ideal. Also remember that you are focusing on learning new and healthy eating habits. If you make healthy eating a natural part of

Learning to eat a healthy, balanced diet is better for your body in the long run than doing fad diets that may not work and don't teach much about everyday nutrition.

your life, you can protect yourself against the dangerous habits that lead to an eating disorder, and you can learn to love your body and the person inside it!

And don't forget to exercise, too. If you don't want to join a gym, take a bike ride or walk or jog in your neighborhood three times every week, or buy exercise videos and work out right at home. The important thing is to focus on all the wonderful things your body can do, not what you think is wrong with it.

If you're concerned about your weight, talk to your parents or your doctor. The doctor can help you plan out a diet and exercise program that's right for you.

How to Fight Bulimia

Although negative body image as portrayed by the media and by society as a whole is hard to avoid, and recovering from bulimia is difficult, it is not impossible to reject those images or to recover from this eating disorder. Remember that many media images are doctored and only represent a small segment of the population. Also remember that people are different, and they should be! You have the power to reject unhealthy and often unattainable body types. Speak out about your concerns, and have conversations about what you see that isn't right. Answer back any person who tells you that you should look a certain way.

Speaking Out

You are a consumer and should feel free to speak out against weight discrimination in the media. Don't like what you see in the latest issue of your favorite magazine? Tell them what you think. If you don't see the changes you want, stop buying it. You can send

The MOM "Mothers & Others" March against eating disorders took place in Washington, DC.

a message to advertisers when you make decisions about what you will and won't support with your money. If you see something on television that upsets you, write a letter to the network. Network executives do care about what viewers think. People often find that fighting against society's messages helps them change their own beliefs. Fighting back can provide a release for all those negative thoughts you may be experiencing.

Reject Diet Culture

People out there are starting to challenge society's thinking about weight. Today, there are e-zines, newsletters, magazines, and books promoting the idea that all body shapes are beautiful. There are many organizations you can join to help fight against diet culture. The National Eating Disorders Association (NEDA) organizes Eating Disorders Awareness Week in February every year. It calls the Friday of that week "Fearless Friday." On that day, everyone has a discussion about healthy eating, and there is even a "smash your scale" event to close out the week.

Choose Positive Self-Talk

Negative self-talk seems to come more easily to people than saying nice things about themselves. It may be short comments like "I feel so fat," or "I should never have eaten that entire candy bar!" But with a little retraining, you can learn how to change negative self-talk to positive. First, try not to focus on what you look like. You probably value your friends for their personalities

Media images have taught people to be hard on themselves for the way that they look. Instead, look for the positive things about yourself and focus on those.

more than their looks. Do the same for yourself. Then try to be aware of the things you say to yourself. Try to catch yourself as you say something negative, and either don't say anything at all or find something positive to say about yourself instead. In fact, make it a point to say a few nice things about yourself every day. Finally, you probably recognize that images in the media contribute to how you feel about your body. Be a critical consumer, and think about what you are looking at. When you remember that most images in magazines are Photoshopped, the image will have less influence over you. You can also choose to be a critical consumer by not purchasing magazines that promote unhealthy body images. Treat yourself as lovingly as you would a friend or family member because you are worth it!

10 GREAT QUESTIONS TO ASK IF YOU THINK YOU HAVE BULIMIA

1. What kinds of tests will I need and what do I need to do to prepare for those tests?

2. What kinds of health problems can I anticipate as a result of my bulimia?

3. Are those problems also treatable and how long will I take to heal?

4. What kind of medication will I have to take and what are the effects of that medication?

5. What treatments are there for me to choose from?

6. How will treatment affect my body?

7. Where can I find out about healthy eating?

8. What kinds of exercise should I be doing and how much?

9. What can I do to control my urge to binge and purge?

10. How can I deal with the emotional causes and effects of this disorder?

GLOSSARY

ADDICTION An obsessive need for or use of a substance or behavior.

AMENORRHEA A condition when a woman who is not pregnant stops getting her period.

ANTIDEPRESSANT A drug prescribed by a medical professional to relieve or prevent depression.

BINGE To eat uncontrollably.

DEHYDRATION The loss of an excessive amount of water or body fluids.

DEPRESSION A feeling of sadness that lasts a long time and may need to be treated with the help of therapy and/or medication.

DISORDER A mental or physical condition or state that is unhealthy.

DIURETIC A drug that increases the amount of urine the kidneys produce.

ELECTROLYTE IMBALANCE A serious condition in which a person doesn't have enough of the minerals necessary for healthy body function.

ESOPHAGUS The tube through which food passes from your throat to your stomach.

ESTROGEN A hormone that occurs naturally in women.

EUPHORIC Feeling great happiness, elation, or well-being.

FASTING Going for a period of time without eating.

GENETIC Related to genes inherited by two parents.

LAXATIVE A substance that brings on a bowel movement.

MENSTRUAL CYCLE Physiological changes in a woman's body from the beginning of one period to the beginning of the next, which includes making of hormones, thickening of the uterine lining, and shedding of the uterine lining that ends with menstrual bleeding (menstruation).

NUTRIENTS Proteins, minerals, and vitamins that a person needs to live and grow.

OSTEOPOROSIS A condition in which the bones become fragile.

PHOTOSHOPPED Altered using a photo editing software such as Photoshop.

PSYCHOLOGICAL Having to do with the mind.

PURGE To clear the body of food, usually through forced vomiting, excessive exercise, or laxatives.

RELAPSE A recurrence of symptoms of a disease or condition after some improvement.

FOR MORE INFORMATION

Anorexia Nervosa and Associated Disorders, Inc. (ANAD)
750 E Diehl Road #127
Naperville, IL 60563
(630) 577-1330
Website: http://www.anad.org
ANAD is a nonprofit group that supports people with eating
disorders in order to educate them and connect them to the
help that they need.

Eating Disorder Hope
(800) 986-4160
Website: http://www.eatingdisorderhope.com
This organization helps support people with eating disorders
through information and by connecting them to health care
professionals. It also features inspirational stories from
celebrities and everyday people talking about their recovery
from bulimia.

Eating Disorders Awareness and Prevention, Inc. (EDAP)
603 Stewart Street, Suite 803
Seattle, WA 98101
(206) 382-3587
Website: http://www.edap.org
This nonprofit organization is dedicated to the elimination of
eating disorders through support, education, training, and
research. EDAP sponsors the National Eating Disorders
Awareness Week.

Eating Disorders Online
Website: http://www.eatingdisordersonline.com

This organization has information about different types of eating
disorders, parent resources, a state-by-state list of facilities,
and a self-test you can take online to gauge if you have an
eating disorder.

Gurl
151 W. 2th Street
New York, NY 10001
(212) 329-8407
Website: http://www.gurl.com
Gurl is an online magazine for young women that talks honestly
about body image.

National Eating Disorders Association (NEDA)
165 West 46th Street, Suite 402
New York, NY 10036
(800) 931-2237
Website: http://www.nationaleatingdisorders.org
NEDA is the largest nonprofit organization that works to prevent
and to help people suffering from bulimia and other eating
disorders.

National Institute of Mental Health (NIMH)
6001 Executive Boulevard, Room 6200, MSC 9663
Bethesda, MD 20892-9663
(866) 615-6464
Website: http://www.nimh.nih.gov
The NIMH helps people learn about all aspects of mental
health, including eating disorders.

Websites

Because of the changing nature of Internet links, Rosen Publishing has developed an online list of websites related to the subject of this book. This site is updated regularly. Please use this link to access the list:

http://www.rosenlinks.com/CED/Bul

Albers, Susan, PsyD. *Eating Mindfully: How to End Mindless Eating and Enjoy a Balanced Relationship with Food.* Oakland, CA: New Harbinger Publications, 2012.

Bacon, Linda. *Health at Every Size: The Surprising Truth About Your Weight.* Dallas, TX: BenBella Books, 2010.

Bulik, Cynthia M. *Crave: Why You Binge Eat and How to Stop.* Columbia, SC: Walker & Company, 2009.

Fairburn, Christopher G. *Overcoming Binge Eating, Second Edition: The Proven Program to Learn Why You Binge and How You Can Stop.* New York, NY: The Guilford Press, 2013.

Fulvio, Leora. *Reclaiming Yourself from Binge Eating: A Step-by-Step Guide.* Alesford, United Kingdom: Ayni Books, 2013.

Gold, Sunny Sea. *Food: the Good Girl's Drug: How to Stop Using Food to Control Your Feelings.* New York, NY: Berkeley, 2011.

Kinzel, Lesley. *Two Whole Cakes: How to Stop Dieting and Learn to Love Your Body.* New York, NY: The Feminist Press at CUNY, 2012.

Koenig, Karen R. *Nice Girls Finish Fat: Put Yourself First and Change Your Eating Forever.* New York, NY: Fireside, 2009.

Koeing, Karen R. *Starting Monday: Seven Keys to a Permanent, Positive Relationship with Food.* Carlsbad, Ca: Gürze Books, 2013.

Ross, Carolyn. *The Binge Eating and Compulsive Overeating Workbook: An Integrated Approach to Overcoming Disordered Eating.* Oakland, CA: New Harbinger Publications, 2009.

Schab, Lisa M. *The Bulimia Workbook for Teens: Activities to Help You Stop Bingeing and Purging.* Oakland, CA: New Harbinger Publications, 2010.

Simon, Julie M. *The Emotional Eater's Repair Manual: A Practical Mind-Body-Spirit Guide for Putting an End to Overeating and Dieting.* Novato, CA: New World Library, 2012.

About the Authors

Ursula Drew is a retired psychologist living in California. She mainly worked with young people who had eating disorders. Drew is also an avid skier and loves to cook.

Stephanie Watson is an award-winning writer based in Atlanta, Georgia. She is a regular contributor to several online and print publications, and she has written or contributed to more than twenty-four books.

Photo Credits